The Daughter of T

Act One

Scene One

In a hospital room Inspector Grant lies in bed with his leg slightly raised in traction. He should be half sitting up so that he can reach objects on the table beside him and the audience can see his upper body. Nurse Ingham is at his side tucking in the sheets, having just tidied up.

Grant: To think that the highlight of my day is you changing the sheets. What has become of me?

Ingham: Well, why don't you read, then? Just look at that lovely pile of books your friends have brought you.

Grant: Have you ever tried reading whilst lying on your back with your leg in traction, Bedbug?

Ingham: It's Nurse Ingham if you don't mind. But I know what you mean.

Grant: Yes, just look at them all. It seems to me that there are far too many books in this world. Anyway, it's damned awkward trying to read but, do you know, I've examined that ceiling for so long I know every single crack by heart. I've explored them all, drawn maps, discovered hidden objects, seen birds, fishes and even faces. I hate the sight of that ceiling, Bedbug. For Heaven's sake, at least turn my bed round a bit so that I've got a new patch to look at.

Ingram: Certainly not. Whatever would Matron say?

Grant: Oh yes, we can't go disturbing the nice symmetry. In a hospital, symmetry is next to cleanliness, with Godliness a poor third.

Ingram: (*Teasing.*) Now, now Inspector Grant. You sound constipated to me. Would you like me to give you something?

Grant: No! Get away from me, Bedbug.

Ingham: (*Exiting, laughing.*) Nurse Ingham!

Grant: (*Calling after her.*) If you see anyone approaching with more books tell them I've died!

Marta Hallard enters.

Marta: Alan? Shall I come another time?

Grant: No, no, Marta, not you. You're always welcome. You are looking very chic.

Marta: Thanks, I'm glad you like it. This will have to be a flying visit; I have rushed over between matinee and evening performance. Here, I brought you some chocolate.

Grant: How lovely.

Marta: And I brought a couple of books, though I feel I shouldn't have bothered.

Grant: I can't read anything.

Marta: Why not? Oh, Alan darling, are you in pain?

Grant: I'm in agony, but it's not my leg.

Marta: What is it then?

Grant: Boredom. I am struck with what my cousin calls "the prickles of boredom".

Marta: Your cousin is correct. One would expect boredom to be a great yawning emotion, but it isn't, of course. It's a small niggling thing.

Grant: It is neither small nor niggling. It is like being beaten with a bunch of nettles.

Marta: What about taking something up? They say that Yoga is very good for the soul.

Grant: Very funny.

Marta: Or I could bring you some wool and knitting needles. You could make yourself some bed socks.

Grant: Your compassion is overwhelming.

Marta: Do you like crosswords? I could bring you a book of those.

Grant: God forbid.

Marta: How about some academic investigating, then? Solving an unsolved problem?

Grant: Crime you mean? Bit of a busman's holiday, isn't it? Besides, I know all the case-histories by heart and there is nothing more that can be done about any of them. Certainly not by someone who is flat on his back.

Marta: I don't mean your Scotland Yard files. I mean something more, what's the word, classic. Something that's puzzled the world for ages.

Grant: Like what?

Marta: I don't know, how about the casket letters?

Grant: God, no. Not Mary, Queen of Scots. I know she's beloved by all you actresses, but I could never be interested in such a silly woman.

Marta: Silly?

Grant: Very silly.

Marta: Oh, Alan, how could you? She was a martyr.

Grant: A martyr to what?

Marta: Her religion.

Grant: The only thing she was a martyr to was rheumatism. She married Darnley without the Pope's dispensation and Bothwell by Protestant rites.

Marta: You will be telling me next that she wasn't even kept prisoner.

Grant: Do you imagine her in a little room at the top of a castle with bars at the window, seeing no one except for the guard who brings her meals? She had a personal household of sixty attendants, all paid for by Elizabeth, who she repaid her by conspiring with European monarchs to try to claim the throne.

Marta: How do you know so much about her?

Grant: I had to do an essay on her at school.

Marta: You didn't like her, I take it.

Grant: I didn't like what I found out about her.

Marta: Not Mary, Queen of Scots, then. How about The Man in the Iron Mask?

Grant: I can't even remember who that was. In any case, I couldn't be interested in anyone who was so coy he hid his face behind some tin plate.

Marta: Oh yes. I suppose faces are important in your line of work. Oh! I think I have just the thing!

Marta takes an envelope out of her bag and hands it to Grant.

Grant: (*Taking several sheets of paper out of the envelope.*) What's this?

Marta: Faces! Dozens of them. Our esteemed director had these printed so that we could study them to help us "get into character".

Grant: How very systematic. Who is this?

Marta: Lucrezia Borgia. Doesn't she look just like a duck?

Grant: Now that you mention it! And who is this Elizabethan gent?

Marta: The name is underneath, Dear.

Grant: Oh, yes. Ah, the Earl of Leicester. Elizabeth's Robin. I don't think I've ever seen his face before.

Marta: Darling, I must fly, or I will be late. How are you, by the way?

Grant: Getting better, apparently.

Marta: Oh, good.

Grant: But I don't see it myself. Until next time, then.

Marta: Take care.

Marta exits passing Ingham on the way in.

Ingham: What a mess. What are all these pictures?

Grant: Faces, Bedbug. Dozens of glorious faces, each with a tale to tell.

Ingham: (*Taking his pulse.*) Your pulse is racing. The effect of a visit from Miss Hallard, no doubt. (*Sticking a thermometer in his mouth and picking up one of the sheets.*) Ooh she's pretty.

Grant: (*Speech effected by having a thermometer in his mouth.*) The Grand Duchess Anastasia.

Ingham: (*Taking out the thermometer.*) Temperatures normal. Anyway. Are you comfortable?

Grant: When is the leg coming down?

Ingham: When Mr. Macfarlane says so. You like faces then?

Grant: They are something of a passion of mine; you can tell so much from a face.

Ingham: You are not trying to tell me that you can spot a criminal just from the way they look?

Grant: No, nothing like that. Crimes are as varied as human nature.

Ingham: Quite. But there are things that can sharpen a face. I've seen that myself.

Grant: Such as?

Ingham: Suffering, for one. Someone who is in pain for long enough, whether physical or mental, it will leave its mark, believe me.

Grant: You're right of course.

Ingham: I mean look at this face (*Picking up a sheet of paper.*) Just look at his eyes! There is a man who has suffered. Or he is constipated.

Grant: You're obsessed with constipation, Bedbug. Pass it here.

Ingham: (*Passing the photo.*) Nurse Ingham. Here.

Grant: Now there's a face for you. What exactly was the artist trying to capture, I wonder? Let's see, about thirty-five, clean shaven. Fifteenth century, I'd say. Obviously, a nobleman of some sort. A prince maybe? Someone who is used to great responsibility. I see what you mean about suffering. Looks like someone who was chronically ill as a child. He's got that special look that childhood suffering leaves behind. But there is something gentle about him.

Ingham: Well? Who is it?

Grant: It doesn't say.

Ingham: (*Picking up another sheet.*) Well, here is a name without a picture so it must belong with that. Oh! Richard III. From the portrait in the National Portrait Gallery. Artist unknown.

Grant: Good heavens. Richard III. The monster of childhood history lessons. Do you think that is what the artist was trying to capture in those eyes? A haunted look. What a portrait this is. It makes the Mona Lisa look like a seaside postcard. What a face! Eyes peering into the middle distance make him look withdrawn; absent minded.

Ingham: Well, it's nice that you've found something to interest you at last, perhaps you will be in a better mood when I see you tomorrow.

Grant: Is it that time already?

Ingham: It most certainly is. I'm just getting off duty and nurse Darrell's right behind me with your tray. See you tomorrow. (*She exits.*)

Grant: Thanks, Bedbug.

Ingham: (*Off.*) Nurse Ingham!

Nurse Darrell enters with a tray.

Grant: Ah, Nurse Darrell. How I've missed you.

Darrell: Go on with you. You haven't given me a moment's thought all day. Who's that you are mooning over? That actress friend of yours?

Grant: No, Nurse Darrell. This is someone who's been dead for hundreds of years. And I'm not mooning. I'm just intrigued. Do you happen to have any history books in your nurse quarters that I could borrow?

Darrell: I do as it happens. I kept all my books from school. I love history. Richard the Lionheart is my favorite.

Grant: Not that brute!

Darrell: Do you want to borrow my books or not?

Grant: I shan't say another word. When do you get off duty?

Darrell: When I finish my trays, but you don't expect me to come traipsing all the way back here with them do you? I'll bring it tomorrow.

Grant: Oh, come on, Nurse Darrell, it will give me something to do this evening. Not even for some chocolate?

Darrell: Hmm. I will think about it. But you are supposed to be resting, not staying up all night reading history books.

Grant: I might as well be looking up history as looking up at the cracks in the ceiling.

Blackout.

Scene Two

The following morning. Grant is asleep with a history book in his hand. Ingham enters.

Ingham: Wakey, wakey rise and shine.

Grant: (*Disorientated at first.*) What! Who's there. Oh, it's you Bedbug.

Ingham: Not like you to have a lie in.

Grant: I can't even remember falling asleep.

Ingham: (*Taking his pulse.*) I see you have changed your mind about reading, then.

Grant: Nurse Darrell was kind enough to bring me something worth reading.

Ingham: (*Reading the title of the book whilst sticking a thermometer in his mouth.*) A History of England. Well, that should keep you busy for a while. What's this one, oh, The Princes in the Tower. I remember that story (*removes the thermometer.*)

Grant: Don't we all?

Ingham: What's brought this on then?

Grant: That picture of Richard III. I wanted to know what can have happened to a man to have shaped a face like his.

Ingham: Well, if it isn't constipation, murdering your own nephews would do it, probably.

Grant: Let me read you a passage (*He picks up The Princes in the Tower.*) "Richard was a man of great ability. But quite unscrupulous as to his means. He claimed the crown on the grounds that his brother's marriage with Elizabeth Woodville had been illegal making the children of it illegitimate. This was accepted by the people, but during his reign the two young princes who were living in the tower disappeared and were believed to be murdered."

Ingham: There you are, then.

Grant: Interesting that it says "believed" to be murdered. It suggests that there wasn't any evidence. And it just says that the princes were living in the tower, not "locked in" or "kept prisoner".

Ingham: Well, I know what I believe. You'd better tidy yourself up. Your favourite nurse will be along in a moment with your breakfast.

Grant: What makes you think that you are not my favourite nurse, Bedbug?

Ingham: (*Laughing.*) Nurse Ingham! Because Nurse Darrell is not the one that has the silly nickname.

Ingham exits. Grant picks up 'The Princes in the Tower' again.

Grant: (*Reading.*) "A serious rebellion followed the disappearance of the two young princes, which Richard put down with great ferocity. A second rebellion followed in the form of an invasion of French, Scottish and Welsh troops led by Henry Tudor. Richard was killed in battle at Bosworth."

Darrell enters with a tray.

Darrell: Talking to yourself?

Grant: Good morning, Nurse Darrell. What do you know about Richard III?

Darrell puts down the tray.

Darrell: Oh, those poor little lambs. I used to have nightmares that someone would put a pillow over my face whilst I was asleep.

Grant: If that is what happened.

Darrell: I know the story well. James Tyrrell made his way to London from the court in Warwick and recruited two thugs on the way. The three of them went to the tower and demanded to see the constable, Sir Robert Brackenbury. They had a royal warrant, you see, which was signed by Richard himself telling the constable to hand over the keys. Brackenbury, the fool, thought the princes were to be released, but Tyrrell had his thugs kill them and bury them under the staircase.

Grant: All very interesting, but it doesn't say any of that in your book

Darrell: Oh, no. Those books are just the history you need to know to pass exams. They don't have any of the interesting stuff.

Grant: So where does this gossip about Tyrrell come from, might I ask?

Darrell: It isn't gossip. You'll find it in Sir Thomas More's History of Richard III, and you can't find a more respected or trustworthy person in the whole of history than Sir Thomas More.

Grant: Who would dare to contradict the Man for all Seasons?

Darrell: Exactly. That's what he wrote in his biography. He was there at the time and knew the right people ask, so I think we have to take his word, don't you?

Grant: I don't suppose you have a copy of this biography?

Darrell: I'm afraid not.

Grant: In that case, I wonder if you might do me a small favour? Would you call Miss Hallard? I can give you the number for the theatre, and ask her to pick up a copy for me.

Darrell: The things I do for you. Here, write on the back of here so I don't forget what it is. (*She passes him the paper containing Richard III's portrait.*)

Grant: Not that, I want to study it some more. (*He props it up on his side table and writes the number on another piece of paper.*)

Darrell: Well, most people have pictures of their family on their side table, but each to his own.

Darrell puts the breakfast tray on Grant's lap exits.
Grant eats his cereal during the following dialogue.
Ingham enters.

Ingham: Can't you find a more cheerful picture than that?

Grant: Don't you find it an interesting face?

Ingham: It gives me the willies.

Grant: According to this book he was a man of great ability.

Ingham: So was Bluebeard.

Grant: And popular with his people.

Ingham: So was Bluebeard.

Grant: And a fine soldier.

Ingham: He was a murdering brute.

Grant: Bluebeard?

Ingham: No. Well, yes. But so was your Richard III. Smothering those children.

Grant: How do you know they were smothered?

Ingham: It was in my history book at school.

Grant: Yes, but who was the book quoting?

Ingham: What do you mean quoting? It's just facts. He sent that Tyrrell to do it. Didn't you do history at school?

Grant: I attended lessons, but that isn't that same thing. How does anyone know it was Tyrrell?

Ingham: He confessed.

Grant: Did he?

Ingham: Yes. Then they hung him.

Grant: You mean that this Tyrrell was hanged for the murder of those two boys?

Ingham: Of course he was. If you are finished, I'll take your tray. Shall I take that picture down and replace it with one of the nicer ones Miss Hallard brought you?

Grant: I'm not interested in nice faces, Bedbug. Only the ones that conceal a story.

Blackout.

Scene Three

The next day. Grant is dozing. Darrell enters holding a book.

Darrell: Miss Hallard left this at reception for you.

Grant: Hmm?

Darrell: I'm sorry. I didn't notice you were sleeping.

Grant: I don't mind if I have something worth waking up for.

Darrell: There's a note.

Grant: (*Reading.*) "Have to send this instead of bringing it. Frantically busy. No T. More in any of the bookshops, so tried Public Library. Can't think why one never thinks of Public Libraries. Probably because books expected to be soupy. Think this looks quite clean and unsoupy. You get fourteen days. Sounds like a sentence rather than a loan." (*Smiling.*) My dear Marta.

Darrell: You've taken my advice then?

Grant: What's that?

Darrell: You've gone to the horse's mouth. Thomas More.

Grant: Don't I always do as I'm told? (*He opens the book at a page at random and reads.*) "He took ill rest at nights, lay long waking and musing; sore wearied with care and watch, he slumbered rather than slept. So was his restless heart continually tossed and tumbled with the tedious impression and stormy remembrance of his most abominable deeds." How extraordinary. (*Continuing to read.*) "This he had from such as were secret with his chamberers." This isn't what I expected at all.

Darrell: How do you mean?

Grant: It reads like servant's gossip. An all too perfect story coming from a biased witness.

Darrell: I'm sure you will find plenty of fact in there. What about the beheading of Lord Hastings? You must remember that from your history lessons.

Whilst Grant is consulting the book, Darrell exits, and Ingham enters. Grant is oblivious to this.

Grant: Oh yes, let's see if I can find it. (*He consults the index.*) Here we are. (*Turning to a page and scanning it.*) Yes. It is all here. That scene in the Tower when he claimed that his deformity was caused by a spell cast by Edward's wife and mistress. Having Hastings, Lord Stanley and John Morton, the Bishop of Ely, arrested before dragging Hastings down to the courtyard and beheading him on a nearby log. (*Turning a few pages.*) Oh, and here is that claim that his brothers, Edward and George, were the result of an affair. That they were illegitimate, and he was the only legitimate offspring of the Duke and Duchess of York. I cannot imagine his mother being thrilled with that story being told, true or not.

Ingham: Well, what did you expect?

Grant: Good God, Bedbug! Where did you spring from? And what have you done with Nurse Darrell?

Ingham: Nurse Darrell has her duties to attend to. As have I. (*She takes his pulse.*)

Grant: Did you know that Richard III was very popular? Before he came to the throne, I mean.

Ingham: He was a snake in the grass if you ask me. Biding his time.

Grant: Biding his time for what? How was he to know that his brother, Edward, would die young? Besides which, there was Edward's large brood of children, including the two princes, as well as George and his children that stood between Richard and the throne.

There is no point in biding your time if there is nothing to bide for.

Ingham: But he murdered everyone who stood in his way. The man was pure evil.

Grant: A few days ago, I might have agreed with you, but there are so many things that don't add up. Take Thomas More.

Ingham: Ooh, no thank you. I prefer my men to be living.

Grant: What is the one thing you know about him?

Ingham: Let's see. Didn't he become a saint?

Grant: Well done, Bedbug. And do you know why?

Ingham: I haven't a clue.

Grant: Because he was executed by Henry VIII for opposing the reformation and refusing to accept him as the head of the English church. The Catholic church made him a saint in the nineteen thirties.

Ingham: There you are then.

Grant: But don't you see? He was executed by Henry VIII, which means that he lived all through Henry VII's reign, after writing the biography of Richard III. Did he live to be one hundred? (*Checking the back of the book.*) "Thomas More – 1478 to 1535". When did Richard die?

Ingham: Why are you asking me?

Grant: Come on, Bedbug. The Battle of Bosworth.

Ingham: I must have missed that lesson.

Grant: 1485, Bedbug. 1485. Thomas More was only seven years old when Richard died. This isn't a contemporary account, at all. He couldn't have interviewed the people involved; it is just hearsay. And if there is one thing that a policeman detests, it is hearsay.

Blackout.

Scene Four

Later that day. Grant is staring at the ceiling, deep in thought. Marta enters.

Marta: Bored with Thomas More already?

Grant: Did you know that he knew nothing about Richard III at all?

Marta: Lovely to see you too. What makes you say that? I thought he was the respected authority.

Grant: He was seven when Richard was killed. Everything in that book is based on what he had been told. Tittle tattle and gossip.

Marta: Oh dear. And the nice man at the library seemed so reverent about him. The Gospel of Richard III according to St Thomas More, and all that.

Grant: Gospel nothing. He was writing down what someone had told him about events that happened when he was five years old. Not the horse's mouth. Not even straight from the course. Come to think of it, it's about as reliable as a bookie's tips would be. He's on the wrong side of the rails altogether. If he was a Tudor servant, he was on opposite side where Richard III was concerned.

Marta: Back to square one then.

Grant: Do you know anyone at the British Museum?

Marta: The BM? I don't think so. Why do you ask?

Grant: They must have some documents. Actual records of events at the time. Facts. That's what I need.

Marta: Atlanta Shergold!

Grant: Who?

Marta: She's in my play. She is the dumb blonde.

Grant: And what does she have to do with the British Museum?

Marta: Not her, but her man, Brent Carradine. He's American too, but we'll forgive him for that. He saw her in Streetcar off Broadway and fell in love.

Grant: He saw her in a streetcar?

Marta: Not a streetcar. I'm sorry, darling, you are the only one of my friends who is not a thespian and I sometimes forget. Brent saw her in 'A Streetcar Named Desire' at a little theatre in New York and became so obsessed he followed her to England where she is in 'To Sea in a Bowl' with me. He can be seen sitting doe eyed in the stalls at every performance.

Grant: What does Miss Shergold make of that?

Marta: She loves it of course.

Grant: I still don't see what this has to do with the British Museum.

Marta: That's where he is when he is not at the theatre. It is some sort of cover story; his father thinks he is here doing research.

Grant: I see.

Marta: Oh, I've made him out to be a love-struck fool, but that is unfair. He is an intelligent young man and he and Atlanta are quite serious. Shall I ask him to call in?

Grant: Thank you, Marta. He could be very useful.

Blackout.

Scene Five

Two days later. Darrell and Grant are in heated debate.

Darrell: But it isn't just Sir Thomas. Everyone describes Richard III as a monster.

Grant: Such as?

Darrell: Shakespeare, for one.

Grant: But that is just a story. Fiction based, no doubt, on the account written by More. No, Nurse Darrell, I am *discontent* with that as an example. (*Darrell groans at this joke.*)

Brent Carradine enters unnoticed.

Darrell: You find me one history book that doesn't say the same thing.

Grant: That is exactly my point. All history books are based on this single account. The sainted More has never been questioned. His reputation has blinded everyone to the cold hard fact that he could not have known what he was writing to be completely accurate. There is nothing in that book that can be called evidence.

Darrell: Nothing? You've read it cover to cover? I only brought it to you two days ago.

Grant: I've read as much as I can stand.

Carradine: (*Hesitantly.*) Um. Excuse me.

Darrell: Oh, you have a visitor. (*To Carradine.*) He is all yours. I can't cope with him in this mood.

Carradine: I'm sorry to disturb you. My name is Carradine.

Grant: Not at all, Mr. Carradine, come in and pull up a chair.

Carradine: Marta, I mean Miss Hallard, said that you wanted something looked up.

Grant: And you are the looker-upper?

Carradine: I'm doing research, here in London. Historical research, I mean. And she said something about your wanting something in that line. She knows

I'm at the museum most mornings. I'd be very pleased, Mr. Grant, to do anything I can to help you.

Grant: That's very kind of you. What is it that you are working on?

Carradine: The Peasant's Revolt.

Grant: Oh, are you interested in social conditions?

Carradine: No, I'm interested in staying in England.

Grant: And you can't without doing research?

Carradine: Not easily. It is my alibi, you see. My father thinks I should go into the family furniture business. We sell it through mail order. Don't get me wrong, it is very good quality, lasts forever. I just don't think furniture is my thing.

Grant: So, you hide away in the British Museum.

Carradine: Well, it's warm and I do like history, but I have to be honest with you. The real reason I am here is because I just had to follow Atlanta Shergold to England. She's the dumb blonde in Miss Hallard's play. I mean, her character is the dumb blonde. There is nothing dumb about Atlanta.

Grant: Indeed. She is very talented.

Carradine: You've seen her?

Grant: Is there anyone left in London who hasn't seen 'To Sea in a Bowl'?

Carradine: It has been a long run, hasn't it? When Atlanta and I waved goodbye to each other in New York we both imagined that she would be back in a few weeks. But, when we found that the run had been extended indefinitely, I just had to come to England.

Grant: Wasn't to be with Atlanta a good enough reason for your father?

Carradine: Not for my Pop! The family are very snooty about Atlanta, but Pop is the worst of the bunch. When he can bring himself to mention her, he refers to her as "that young actress acquaintance of yours." You see, Pop is "Carradine The Third", and Atlanta's father is very much Shergold the First. A little grocery store on Main Street, as a matter of fact. And the salt of the earth, in case you're interested. And of course, Atlanta hadn't really done very much in the states other than that little part of the nurse in Streetcar, and that was in a tiny theatre off Broadway. This is her first big success. That is why she didn't want to break her contract and come back home.

Grant: So, you took up research.

Carradine: It's perfect. I enjoy doing it and it keeps Pop happy. Who's that? (*He points to the portrait of Richard III.*)

Grant: Richard III.

Carradine: Can I see?

Grant: Of course.

Carradine: (*Picking up the portrait and studying it.*) You're the first I've met who has a king for a pin-up.

Grant: He's no beauty, is he?

Carradine: Oh, I don't know. He looks a bit like a college professor of mine. Poor chap suffers with chronic indigestion but he's the kindest person imaginable. Is this who you want me to look up?

Grant: Yes. Nothing too arduous, I just want to know what a contemporary authority has to report.

Carradine: That shouldn't be too difficult. It is not far from the period I'm studying already. In fact, the current authority, Cuthbert Oliphant, covers both periods. I've a copy in my bag, as it happens. Have you read Oliphant?

Grant: I haven't. Just schoolbooks and Thomas More.

Carradine: More? Henry VII's chancellor?

Grant: That's him.

Carradine: I take you are not happy with his account.

Grant: It read like a publicity pamphlet for the Tudors. No, actually, worse than that. More like something you would read in a scandal sheet such as the News of the World. Downstairs gossip masquerading as journalism.

Carradine: That bad, eh?

Grant: Do you know much about Richard III?

Carradine: Only that he murdered his nephews and offered his kingdom for a horse. Oh yes, and he had two stooges. The Cat and the Rat.

Grant: The Cat and the Rat?

Carradine: The Cat, the Rat, and Lovell the Dog, Rule all England under a Hog.

Grant: I haven't heard that since I was a schoolboy and I'm amazed it made its way across the Atlantic. Would does it mean?

Carradine: I haven't a clue. It must be something to do with Richard's royal crest being a pig, but it's just something history students say to show off whenever his name was mentioned. What got you interested in him, anyway?

Grant: It was Marta. She suggested I could pass my time by solving a mystery, and he has turned out to be the biggest mystery of the lot.

Carradine: How do you mean?

Grant: His notoriety comes from the most revolting crime in all of history, yet all accounts suggest that he was a civilized and well-liked creature. Before he came to the throne he was celebrated as a great administrator in the north of England and a first-class soldier. He was also known to have been devoted to his brother Edward. So, what turned him into the monster that murdered Edward's children?

Carradine: Perhaps he hated Edward but hid it well. Edward was tall and handsome, Richard small with a hunchback and withered arm. Plenty of reason for resentment.

Grant: It's possible. That's the best explanation I've heard so far, anyway.

Carradine: It's interesting what you say about him apparently being a good sort until the crime. Makes him seem real. The Shakespeare version is more of a caricature. I'll be glad to do any investigation you want, Mr. Grant. It will make a nice change from the peasants.

Grant: That's very kind of you. I'm most interested in reading contemporary accounts of the murder. It must have rocked the country, so there should be plenty to choose from.

Carradine: I'll see what I can rake up. Would you like me to leave Oliphant with you?

Grant: If you are sure you don't mind.

Carradine: Not at all. (*He takes the book out of his bag and passes it to Grant.*) Well, I will call again in a couple of days. Hopefully I will have plenty for you by then. Goodbye, Mr. Grant.

Grant: Goodbye, Brent.

Carradine exits. Blackout.

Scene Six

A few days later. Marta is thumbing through Oliphant.

Marta: It looks completely indigestible. Apart from him dumping this on you, what did you think of Brent Carradine?

Grant: It was very kind of you to find him for me.

Marta: I didn't have to find him. He's continually underfoot. He practically lives at the theatre. He must have seen 'To Sea in a Bowl' five hundred times and when he's not out front, he is in Atlanta's dressing room. I wish they'd get married, and then we might see less of him.

Grant: That bad?

Marta: No, I'm being mean. They're really rather sweet together. In some ways they are more like twins than lovers. They have that utter trust in each other; that dependence on the other half to make a proper whole. Perhaps I am just jealous. So, is this tombstone worth the effort.

Grant: A bit unappetising, but quite easily digested once you have swallowed it. History for the student. Set out in detailed fact.

Marta: Ugh!

Grant: At least I've discovered where the sainted Sir Thomas More got his account of Richard.

Marta: Oh? Where?

Grant: Someone called John Morton.

Marta: Never heard of him.

Grant: Neither had I. He was Henry VII's Archbishop of Canterbury and a bitter enemy of Richard III.

Marta: Not an unbiased account then.

Grant: Not at all. And it is on that account of Richard that all the later ones were built. It is what is in our history books and what Shakespeare used in his Tragedy.

Marta: So, anything that anyone knows about Richard is based on an account written by someone who hated him. Why on Earth did Thomas More choose him?

Grant: From what I understand, More lived in the Morton household for a while as he was growing up. I suppose he just swallowed it all unquestionably.

Marta: Does Oliphant acknowledge the bias?

Grant: Not exactly. He seems to be in as big a muddle about the whole thing as I am myself. On one page he'll say that Richard was admired and popular, and on the next that he was unscrupulous and violent.

Marta: I take it that Mr. Oliphant preferred his roses to be red.

Grant: I don't think so, not consciously, anyway. Though he does seem very tolerant of Henry VII. Nowhere does he mention that Henry had not the slightest claim to the throne.

Marta: Who put him there?

Grant: Well, the Lancastrians who survived the Battle of Bosworth, of course. And backed by the House of Woodville.

Marta: Who?

Grant: Elizabeth Woodville was married to Richard's predecessor, his brother, Edward. And was the mother to the princes in the tower.

Marta: I'm getting a bit lost. The princes were illegitimate, is that right? That's why they didn't inherit the crown.

Grant: Yes, because Edward's marriage to Elizabeth Woodville was invalid. He was already married to another woman, Elizabeth Lucy.

Marta: Well, that was rather silly of him. All that aside, are you any closer to discovering what sort of a man Richard III was?

Grant: I'm about as confused as Oliphant. The difference is that I know I'm confused, whilst he doesn't seem to be aware of it.

Carradine enters.

Carradine: Oh, excuse me. I didn't know you were here, Miss Hallard.

Marta: That's all right, Brent. I was just about to leave. In any case, I think you are a more welcome visitor than myself just at the moment.

Grant: Heavens, no.

Marta: That's kind of you, Alan, but I can see the bit between your teeth. I'll leave you two in peace.

Marta exits.

Carradine: How are you getting on with Oliphant?

Grant: I find him very articulate, if a little muddled. I discovered who the Cat and the Rat were, by the way.

Carradine: Oh?

Grant: William Catesby, Speaker of the House of Commons, and Richard Ratcliffe, one of Richard's knights. Incidentally, I'm afraid Oliphant has de-bunked your theory about why Richard hated his brother, Edward. According to Oliphant, Richard had no deformity whatsoever. The hunchback and withered arm were a complete myth.

Carradine: That's interesting.

Grant: Did you find a contemporary historian for me?

Carradine: There isn't one.

Grant: None at all?

Carradine: Not in the sense that you mean it. There were writers who were contemporaries of Richard, but they didn't write anything about the murder of the boys until after Richard's death when they were living under a Tudor monarchy. Therefore, anything they say must be taken with a pinch of salt. There is a chronicle written by a monk in Latin which is contemporary, but I haven't managed to get hold of it yet.

Grant: Keep looking, will you.

Carradine: Of course. One thing that I did discover that is rather interesting. The Biography of Richard III is not one of Thomas More's published works. It has been credited to him because the unfinished manuscript was found amongst his papers, but it was just a handwritten copy of somebody else's account.

Grant: Now, that is interesting. Oliphant says that More got his account of Richard III from John Morton, so it is reasonable to assume that the original work that More was copying had been originally written by Morton. That would explain the below stairs gossip. Do you know about Morton?

Carradine: I don't think I do.

Grant: He was a lawyer turned clergyman. Edward made him Bishop of Ely and God knows how many parishes besides, then Henry VII made him Archbishop of Canterbury.

Carradine: Wait a minute, I do know him. He's the Morton of Morton's Fork.

Grant: That was another of his roles. Henry's tax collector.

Carradine: If you are not spending much money, you must have some put aside for the king, if you are spending freely then you must be able to afford some for the king.

Grant: Exactly. And I've just thought of a reason why Morton will have hated Richard that has nothing to do with the princes in the tower. Edward had taken a bribe from King Louis XI to form a dishonorable peace. When Richard came to power, he wanted nothing to do with it and refused the cash, much of it destined to Morton. There is no wonder Morton sided with the Woodvilles.

Carradine: I wanted to ask you something about the princes in the tower.

Grant: Yes.

Carradine: Don't you think it is odd that no one talks about the murder?

Grant: What do you mean, no one talks about it?

Carradine: For the last three days, since I last saw you, I have been going though contemporary papers, letters, etc. There is no mention of the princes in the tower being murdered. What's more, after Bosworth, Henry brought a bill before parliament accusing Richard of all and sundry. Cruelty, tyranny, you name it. He throws the book at Richard accusing him of everything under the sun, but he does not mention the murder of the princes.

Grant: What?

Carradine: Surprising, isn't it?

Grant: It is more than surprising. It doesn't make any sense. He must have gone to the tower as soon as he got back to London. There is no possible explanation for him not publicising the fact that they were missing.

Carradine: Unless they weren't missing.

Grant: But that is fantastic.

Carradine: I've been looking at it for three days, and I can't come up with any other reason.

Grant: You are sure of this. There is no record of anyone accusing Richard of murdering the boys at the time of Henry's assent to the throne.

Carradine: None at all.

Grant: But wait a moment. Tyrrell was hanged for it! Even Darrell knew that. Let's see what Oliphant says. (*He picks up the book, looks in the index and starts to thumb through.*)

Carradine: Darrell who?

Grant: Nurse Darrell. If you haven't come across her yet, you are in for a treat. Here we are. He was tried and found guilty, and he confessed before being executed. Good God!

Carradine: What is it?

Grant: In 1502!

Carradine: What?

Grant: 1502. Twenty years after the event. What in God's name is going on? We've been going about this the wrong way, Carradine. The truth of anything doesn't lie in someone's account of it. It lies in facts. A receipt. A document. A contract. Evidence.

Carradine: This is the first time I've heard you sound like a policeman.

Grant: That's because I am finally thinking like a policeman. I'm asking myself the question that every policeman asks in every case of murder: Who benefits? And for the first time it occurs to me that the theory that Richard got rid of the boys to make himself safer on the throne is nonsense. Supposing he had got rid of the boys. There were still the boys' five sisters between him and the throne. To say nothing of his other brother's children. If Richard believed his claim to the throne to be shaky, there were many more than just those two princes that he would need to murder in order to put him first in line.

Carradine: Did they all survive?

Grant: I don't know, but that is for us to find out. Certainly, his brother's daughter, Elizabeth, did because she married Henry.

Carradine: Let's go back to the beginning. As you said yourself, we need facts. Evidence. Let's forget about the history books or anyone's opinion. The truth does not lie in accounts, but in account books.

Grant: That's a nice phrase. What does it mean?

Carradine: Real history is written in forms not meant as history. In Wardrobe accounts, in Privy Purse expenses, in personal letters, in estate books. If someone insists that Lady Whoosit never had a child, but you find in the account book the entry that says: "For the son born to my lady: five yards of blue ribbon at fourpence halfpenny" it's a reasonably fair deduction that my lady had a child after all.

Grant: You're right. So where do we begin?

Carradine: You are the investigator. I'm just the looker upper.

Grant: Researcher.

Carradine: Researcher. Thank you. What do you want to know?

Grant: We should start with the thing that set everything into motion. The death of King Edward IV. It was unexpected so it must have caught people on the hop. How did people react?

Carradine: Meaning what did they do, rather than what did they think.

Grant: Exactly.

Carradine: I'll get on to it straightaway. Thank you, Mr. Grant. This is a lot more interesting than peasants.

Blackout.

Scene Seven

Ingham is doing the vitals.

Ingham: I see you've still got that horrible picture stood up there. The thing has become an obsession with you. Every time I come in you are staring at it or at the ceiling. You are not even bothering with your books anymore, it seems.

Grant: I've had it with history books, Bedbug. I'm waiting for Mr. Carradine to return with more reliable information.

Ingham: Is that the nice young American who has been visiting you? I might hang around to see if I can bump into him again.

Grant: He's taken I'm afraid, Bedbug. I'm hoping he will call this morning though. It has been three days.

Ingham: Poor you. Are you missing your little pal?

Grant: It is nice to have someone I can have an intelligent conversation with. What would you say if I told you that the Bill of Attainder brought against Richard didn't mention the princes in the tower?

Ingham: I'd say what is a Bill of Attainder?

Grant: Precisely my point.

Ingham: Well don't bother enlightening me, I'm not interested.

Grant: But with Richard dead and his followers on the run, why on earth not make any reference to his most heinous crime?

Ingham: I'm sure there must be some explanation.

Grant: Well, of course there is an explanation. I just don't know what it is!

Carradine enters.

Ingham: Well, you are in luck. Your friend has returned.

Ingham exits with a cheeky wink aimed at Carradine.

Grant: Thank God. Intelligent conversation at last!

Carradine: Good morning, Mr. Grant.

Grant: You seem quite chipper.

Carradine: I have much to be chipper about.

Grant: Come on then, don't keep me in suspense.

Carradine: So. Starting with Edward. He died on April 9th, 1483, in London. With him were his queen, daughters and the younger prince. The older prince, the heir to the throne, was at Ludlow with the queen's brother, Lord Rivers, otherwise known as Anthony Woodville. She did seem to have a huge number of relations; you could hardly move for the Woodville clan.

Grant: Yes, I know. So where was Richard at the time?

Carradine: Scotland.

Grant: Really?

Carradine: Yes, he is way off base. But does he call for a horse and charge down to London? No, he does not. Instead, he makes his way to York where he holds a requiem mass and gets the great and the good to swear an oath of loyalty to the older prince.

Grant: The assumed heir to the throne.

Carradine: Exactly.

Grant: What does Rivers, the queen's brother, do?

Carradine: He sets off from Ludlow with the prince and two thousand armed soldiers.

Grant: I see. And did Richard also head south with an army?

Carradine: No. He made his way to Northampton in the company of around six hundred gentry, but they were not armed. He'd expected to meet the crowd from Ludlow there, but they had already gone on without him to Stoney Stratford. He was met, however, by the Duke of Buckingham who brought soldiers and news from London.

Grant: What news?

Carradine: That I cannot tell you but, whatever it was, it was enough to persuade Richard to make haste to Stoney Stratford, have Rivers arrested and accompany the prince to London himself.

Grant: Well, there must have been something that troubled him about Rivers because, that aside, it all fits the pattern of the respected and well-liked Richard that we know. He mourns the death of the king and swears allegiance to the heir. When did it all change?

Carradine: Not for several months. When Henry arrived in London, he found that the boy's mother had taken her family into sanctuary at Westminster Abbey. But we cannot say for certain what prompted that action or who she feared.

Grant: Did Richard take the young heir to the tower.

Carradine: No, he took him to the Bishop's Palace at St Paul's. Richard himself went to stay with his mother until his wife arrived on June 5th when they went to live at Crosby Place.

Grant: No hint of any trouble?

Carradine: None that I can find. He is named on two official documents from the exact time as being the boy's protector. And on the day his wife arrived in London he set the date for the boy's coronation. June 22nd.

Grant: That didn't give him a lot of time to make a challenge for the throne.

Carradine: There is nothing to suggest that he intended to do so. There were invitations for the coronation sent to various knights of the realm and I even found an order for the boy's coronation clothes. But everything changed on June 8th when Stillington, the Bishop of Bath, broke some news.

Grant: Which was?

Carradine: That he had presided over the marriage of Edward IV to Lady Eleanor Butler before Edward went on to marry Elizabeth Woodville, making the second marriage bigamous and illegitimate.

Grant: Butler?

Carradine: Yes?

Grant: But that's not right according to More?

Carradine: Oh no. Not the sainted More, again.

Grant: Hold on. (*He searches the index then the book.*) Yes. It says here that Richard claimed Edward had previously been married to his mistress, Elizabeth Lucy, but there was no evidence to support this claim. Why would More say it was Elizabeth Lucy when it was Eleanor Butler? You have evidence of this happening? Not just talk.

Carradine: I do. On June 9th a report was prepared for parliament. On June 10th Richard sent a letter to York asking for troops. On June 11th he sent a similar letter to Lord Neville so he clearly felt that he was in danger. Then, on June 20th he took some guards with him to the Tower of London. Did you know that the tower was just a residence? Not a prison at all.

Grant: Yes, I knew that. Why did Richard go there?

Carradine: To interrupt a meeting of conspirators. Lord Hastings, Lord Stanley and one John Morton, the Bishop of Ely.

Grant: Ah, Morton. I knew we'd get to him eventually.

Carradine: There was, apparently, a plot to murder Richard but, to be fair, I can find no record of it. Only one of the conspirators was be-headed though.

Grant: Ah yes. Lord Hastings. They rushed him down to the courtyard and chopped his head off on the nearest log.

Carradine: Rushed, nothing. It was a week later.

Grant: What happened to Lord Stanley and John Morton?

Carradine: Well, Stanley was pardoned.

Grant: Oh no.

Carradine: What's wrong?

Grant: Stanley and his troops switched allegiance to Henry at Bosworth. To think, if Richard hadn't pardoned him, he might have won at Bosworth, and we would have never had a Tudor monarchy or stories about an evil hunchback. What about Morton?

Carradine: Nothing.

Grant: Nothing?

Carradine: Nothing. Well, nothing of significance. He was put under detention under Lord Buckingham, but I don't think it would have been much of a hardship. It was just Hastings and Lord Rivers who went to the block. It strikes me to Richard was trying to put an end to the quarrelling between the houses of York and Lancaster.

Grant: What makes you say that?

Carradine: His coronation was very well attended from both houses. No one stayed away.

Grant: Yes, and I suppose there was his leniency to Lord Stanley too.

Carradine: Was Stanley Lancastrian then?

Grant: No, but his wife was. A particularly rabid one. Margaret Beaufort was her name. Henry's mother.

Carradine: Henry VII?

Grant: Yes.

Carradine: Wow! But she had a place of honour at Richard's coronation.

Grant: Poor Richard. So parliament accepted Stillington's version of events.

Carradine: They did more than that. They incorporated it into an act: Titulus Regius. It declared the princes illegitimate and gave Richard the crown. Here's another thing of interest. Henry had it destroyed when he came to the throne. He didn't just repeal it. He ordered all copies to be destroyed. Anyone found with a copy was imprisoned.

Grant: What of the queen? Did she stay in sanctuary?

Carradine: Yes, but she let her youngest boy go to join his brother where they lived at the tower. Lived at, not imprisoned at.

Grant: Let's stop and think for a moment. We know that More's account, the once that states that Richard claimed Edward had married Elizabeth Lucy, was actually written by John Morton who was there at the time and knew very well that the Titulus Regius named Eleanor Butler, not Elizabeth Lucy. That means we have Henry destroying the Titulus Regius leaving the door open for Morton to mislead on what it said.

Carradine: That's right.

Grant: But I still don't see why it mattered to Henry. Henry was Lancaster. Where Richard was in line to the throne on the York side, makes no difference to Henry.

Ingham enters.

Ingham: Ooh. (*She smiles shyly at Carradine.*) Don't mind me. I forgot to record your pulse, Mr. Grant. (*She takes his pulse. Meanwhile, Carradine picks up More's book and studies it.*)

Grant: What would say if I told you that Richard III didn't murder anyone, Bedbug?

Ingham: Nurse Ingham. I'd say that you're perfectly entitled to your opinion. Some people believe the earth is flat. Some people believe the world is going to end in A.D. 2000. Some people believe that it began less than five thousand years ago. You'll hear far funnier things than that at Marble Arch of a Sunday.

Grant: So, you wouldn't even entertain the idea for a moment?'

Ingham: I find it entertaining all right, but not what you might call very plausible. But don't let me stand in your way. Take it to Marble Arch one Sunday, and I'll bet you'll find followers aplenty. Maybe start a movement. You pulse is normal, at least. (*She smiles again at Carradine and exits.*)

Carradine: I was just wondering what happened to Morton after Richard had him arrested. Given that this was actually written by Morton you would think he'd know. All it says is that he escaped from Lord Buckingham and lived back in Ely for a while before heading to France.

Grant: I was also doing some thinking whilst Bedbug was twittering about. If Henry had all copies of Titulus Regius destroyed, how do you know what it said?

Carradine: He missed the original draft. It didn't turn up until 1611 when it was found, by chance, in the Tower records.

Grant: So, there's no question at all about Titulus Regius. The sainted More's account is nonsense. There never was an Elizabeth Lucy in the matter.

Carradine: The princes were illegitimate and Richard's claim to the throne was valid.

Grant: And from a policeman's point of view that means there was no motive.

Carradine: I'll tell you another thing. Edward's widow and her daughters came out of sanctuary not long after Richard's coronation. It is as though they felt safe now that he was on the throne. This coming after the time that he was supposed to have murdered her boys. She even let her daughters attend festivities at the palace. And then she writes to her other son, from her previous marriage, asking him to make peace with Richard. I'm no policeman, but as far as I can see, for as long as Richard lived, the young princes were alive and well.

Grant: Well, I am a policeman and I say that there is no case against Richard. I don't just mean there isn't enough to take him to court. There isn't a case against him at all.

Carradine: Incredible.

Grant: But unfortunately...

Carradine: What?

Grant: As a policeman...

Carradine: Yes.

Grant: I still have to answer the real question.

Carradine: What is that?

Grant: If Richard didn't murder the boys, then who did?

Blackout.

Act Two

Scene Eight

Grant is sitting in a chair by his bed reading Oliphant. Marta enters.

Marta: Oh, Alan. How wonderful. You are up!

Grant: Yes, it took two nurses and a porter to get me into the chair and it will probably take a small army to get me back into the bed, but it is nice to be up. How are you, darling?

Marta: I'm just fine. I see you are still engrossed in Oliphant.

Grant: I'm doing what every good policeman does. Checking and re-checking my theory. Although it does seem pretty conclusive. If your two sons had been murdered by your brother-in-law, would you take a pension from him?

Marta: I take it that the question is rhetorical.

Grant: I honestly think historians are all mad. Listen to this: "The conduct of the Queen Dowager is hard to explain; whether she feared to be taken from sanctuary by force, or whether she was merely tired of her forlorn existence at Westminster and had resolved to be reconciled to the murderer of her sons out of mere callous apathy, seems uncertain."

Marta: Good Heavens!

Grant: I wonder if historians ever listen to themselves. By the way, you can take Thomas More back to the library. I never want to see him again.

Marta: (*Putting the book in her bag.*) The Queen Dowager was the boys' mother?

Grant: Yes, Elizabeth Woodville. I mean, perhaps I have lived a sheltered life, but where on Earth would you find a mother who was prepared to become pally with the murderer of her children?

Marta: Ancient Greece, perhaps.

Grant: Not even there, surely.

Marta: I played her, you know, in Richard III. To think Shakespeare wrote it as a tragedy. It is more like a farce.

Grant: You are right. It's absurd. Oliphant doesn't seem to consider how likely it is that what he is writing actually happened. And he is one of the more trustworthy historians. How did you play her?

Marta: With venom. I refer to Richard as a bottled spider and a foul hunchbacked toad. I rather enjoyed that line. Every night I tried to catch the eye of the director as I said it.

Grant: How can Oliphant suggest that she feared being forced out of sanctuary. That never happened. Whoever tried it would be excommunicated. No, she left willingly, for sure.

Marta: How do you explain it?

Grant: The obvious explanation is that the boys were alive and well. No one at that time ever suggested otherwise.

Marta: Well, you and Brent seem to be having a good old time. The little pastime I suggested to ease the prickles of boredom seems to have resulted in you re-writing history! Oh, that reminds me. Atlanta Shergold is angry with you.

Grant: Why? I've never even met her.

Marta: No, but you have stolen Brent from her. We hardly see him at the theatre now.

Grant: Well, I believe we are coming to the end of our investigation. You can assure Miss Shergold that she'll get her man back before very long.

Marta: I'm sure she will be pleased. (*Carradine enters.*) Oh. We were just talking about you.

Grant: Speak of the devil. (*Seeing Carradine's solemn expression.*) Is something wrong?

Carradine: Everything's wrong. We are undone. Oh, you are out of bed.

Grant: Never mind that, what's happened?

Carradine: A terrible thing. You know that chronicle written in Latin I talked about, the one written by the monk at Croyland Abbey, well I got hold of it and it mentions there being a rumour that the boys are dead. And this thing was written whilst Richard was still alive. It is a contemporary account.

Grant: Damn and blast. It might just be a rumour, but it is enough to throw our theory into doubt.

Carradine: It gets worse. I spent a little time looking to see if there was any other mention of this rumour, and I turned up a another. This time it was the Chancellor of France in a speech to his assembly. My French is not so good, so I copied it out for you to read yourself, but the meaning seems quite clear. (*He hands Grant a sheet of paper.*)

Grant: Would you oblige, Marta? (*He passes it to Marta.*)

Marta: (*Reading*) La nouvelle nous est parvenue que les enfants d'Edward ont été massacrés et que la couronne a été décernée à l'assassin. It says, "News has reached us that Edward's children have been massacred and the crown has been awarded to the assassin" Oh dear.

Carradine: We're sunk.

Grant: It does seem that way.

Marta: I'm so sorry. Croyland Abbey is so beautiful as well. It doesn't feel right that such a lovely place is the source of your downfall.

Grant: You've been there?

Marta: Yes. It is in Cambridgeshire or Norfolk or somewhere round there. Not far from Peterborough.

Carradine: Wherever is it, I loathe the place.

The three of them sit in solemn silence for a moment.

Grant: (*Suddenly.*) Ely!

Marta: What?

Grant: Ely. It is close to Ely.

Marta: Yes, I suppose it is.

Carradine: Good God!

Grant: Do you have the dates of those documents?

Carradine: I do. The monk wrote his account in late summer 1483 and the address to the assembly was in January 1484. It fits!

Marta: I'm confused. What fits?

Grant: Richard's bitterest enemy was John Morton, Bishop of Ely. He was at the heart of a conspiracy to murder Richard before he was crowned and was arrested in June 1483. We know that he escaped in the summer of that year and hid somewhere near his old stomping ground of Ely, before escaping to France in the autumn. That's what fits.

Marta: I see. So, there is no truth in it.

Carradine: Unless the rumour turns up elsewhere.

Grant: That is highly unlikely. If the rumour was in general circulation, then Richard would have stamped on it. After all, when there was a story going round that he wanted to marry his niece, the boys' elder sister, he immediately quashed it. And marrying one's niece was quite the done thing in those days, no one would have batted an eyelid. If he took such immediate and decisive action to quash that rumour, then he would have leapt on any story that he had murdered the boys right away.

Marta: Unless the rumour was true.

Grant: Unless the rumour was true, but in that case, there would be a public record of it. The conclusion is inevitable: there was no general rumour of disappearance or foul play where the boys were concerned.

Carradine: That's a relief.

Grant: Nothing in the picture suggests any worry about the boys. I mean, in a police investigation you look for any abnormalities in behaviour among the suspects in a crime. Why did X, who always goes to the cinema on a Thursday night, decide not to go on that particular night? Why did Y buy a return ticket as usual but not make the return journey? That sort of thing. But in the short time between Richard's succession and his death everyone behaves quite normally.

The boys' mother comes out of sanctuary and makes her peace with Richard. The girls resume their court life. The boys are presumably still doing the lessons that their father's death had interrupted. Their young cousins have a place on the Council and are of sufficient importance for the town of York to be addressing letters to them. It's all quite a normal, peaceful scene, with everyone going about their ordinary business, and no suggestion anywhere that a spectacular and unnecessary murder has just taken place in the family.

Marta: It is wonderful to hear you talking like a policeman once again. You are clearly on the mend.

Grant: A question a policeman always asks is who benefits? We know that the boy's death gave Richard no advantage whatsoever. So, who would benefit? That is where Titulus Regius comes in.

Marta: What is Titulus Regius?

Grant: The act of parliament that declared Richard King. It stated that Edward's marriage to Elizabeth was invalid, and their children were, therefore, illegitimate. Henry VII had all copies of it destroyed, or so he thought. A copy turned up centuries later.

Marta: What does Titulus Regius have to do with the murder?

Grant: Henry married the boys' sister.

Marta: Yes.

Grant: In order to reconcile the House of York to his occupation of the throne.

Marta: Yes.

Grant: By repealing and destroying Titulus Regius, he made her legitimate.

Marta: Yes.

Grant: But by making the children legitimate he automatically made the two boys heir to the throne before her. In fact, by repealing Titulus Regius he effectively made the elder of the two King of England.

Marta: Goodness! I think I see what you are saying.

Carradine: It is as clear as day. Henry was the one who benefited from the boy's death.

Ingham enters.

Ingham: It is like Piccadilly Circus in here. Off with you. I need to see to my patient.

Grant: Oh, go away, Bedbug.

Ingham: It's Nurse Ingham. And you are not at Scotland Yard now. This is a hospital and I'm responsible for looking after you.

Grant: Can't you come back later? We are just on the point of something important.

Ingham: And so am I. I need to record your vitals.

Grant: I'm fine, will that do?

Ingham: No. Come along, Mr. Grant.

Marta: You are quite right, Nurse Ingham. We are just leaving.

Marta takes Carradine by the elbow and leads him to the exit.

Grant: (*Shouting after Carradine.*) Find out everything you can about Tyrrell. Who he was and what he'd done.

Carradine: Righto.

Grant: (*Still shouting after Carradine.*) And what became of all those York heirs that Richard left alive and well. Can you do that?

Carradine: (*Off.*) Sure thing.

Grant: (*To Ingham.*) Now then my dear Nurse Ingham. I'm all yours.

Ingham: That's better.

Blackout.

Scene Nine

Grant is sat in his chair. Nurse Darrell is tucking a blanket under his legs.

Grant: I really don't think that is necessary, you know.

Darrell: We don't want you catching cold. Not when you are nearly ready to go home.

Grant: I feel I could walk out of here now.

Darrell: You probably could but considering the amount of time it has just taken you to walk to the window and back, I think it would be dark before you reached the hospital gate. Be patient. Just a few more days.

Grant: Perhaps my release will coincide with me solving the case.

Darrell: The case?

Grant: Richard III.

Darrell: Oh, you're still on that are you?

Grant: You remember that gossip about Tyrrell.

Darrell: I remember telling you that it wasn't gossip.

Grant: When do you suppose he was executed for the boys' murder.

Darrell: When Henry came to the throne I suppose.

Grant: It wasn't for another twenty years.

Darrell: Perhaps Henry never knew it was him.

Grant: That seems unlikely.

Darrell: Well, I've got better things to worry about. I'll leave you to it.

Darrell exits. Grant picks up the picture and studies it. Carradine enters.

Carradine: Still puzzling over the face? I was just thinking it would make an excellent cover for a book.

Grant: You're not thinking of writing one, are you?

Carradine: Unless you wanted to.

Grant: God forbid.

Carradine: I thought it would be something to show Pop. He is so exasperated because I have no interest in furniture and graphs that show sales over a financial period. I thought that, if I could get a book published, he might not think me so useless after all.

Grant: What would you call it.

Carradine: I might borrow a phrase from Henry Ford. History is Bunk.

Grant: Very apt.

Carradine: You've no objections then?

Grant: Write away. But before that, tell me what you have found out about the Yorks. How did they make out under Henry VII?

Carradine: Oh yes. Where shall we begin.

Grant: Well, we know about the boy's sister, Edward's eldest daughter, that is. Henry married her.

Carradine: Yes, they were married in 1486 and she died in 1503.

Grant: Seventeen years. The poor thing, it must have felt like seventy. Fate of the boys unknown. What about the others?

Carradine: Cecily was married off and went to live in Lincolnshire. Anne and Katherine, when they were old enough, were married to good solid Lancastrians and Bridget became a nun.

Grant: Nothing unusual there. What other Yorks were there?

Carradine: (*Consulting a piece of paper.*) Warwick was locked up in the Tower and executed when he tried to escape. John de la Pole went to live with his aunt in Burgundy.

Grant: Richard's sister?

Carradine: Yes. He died in the Simnel Rebellion against Henry. His younger brother surrendered to Henry but was later executed by Henry VIII. There are four more. Lords Exeter, Surrey, Buckingham and Montague. Henry got rid of the lot.

Grant: How about Richard's illegitimate son, John?

Carradine: He was the first to go.

Grant: What was the charge?

Carradine: An invitation to go to Ireland.

Grant: You're joking.

Carradine: I'm not. The York family were popular in Ireland.

Grant: So.

Carradine: So.

Grant: Are you thinking what I'm thinking?

Carradine: Only two male heirs unaccounted for. The rest were executed, imprisoned or died in battle against Henry.

Grant: Executions are legal. But you cannot execute children.

Carradine: No.

Grant: And those two boys were the most important. They were the direct descendants to the throne. They would have to be got rid of some other way.

Carradine: Where do we start?

Grant: The same as we did for Richard. We find out where everybody was and what they were doing in the first six months of Henry's reign and look for a break to the pattern.

Carradine: Right.

Grant: What did you find out about Tyrrell?

Carradine: He wasn't at all what I expected. I thought he would be some sort of goon. A hanger on.

Grant: Wasn't he?

Carradine: No, he was a very important person. Sir James Tyrrell. He sat on lots of committees under Edward and did well for himself under Richard.

Grant: And how did he fare under Henry?

Carradine: Well, that is the really interesting thing. For such a good and successful servant of the York family, he seems to have fairly blossomed under Henry VII. Henry appointed him Constable of Calais. then he was sent as ambassador to Rome. He was given a grant for life. Things were going very well for him until 1502.

Grant: What happened then?

Carradine: Word got to Henry that Tyrrell was plotting the escape of one of the York crowd from the tower. He was brought back from Calais and beheaded without trial.

Grant: He was beheaded for plotting against Henry?

Carradine: Yes.

Grant: Not for the murder of the boys?

Carradine: No mention of it.

Grant: But he confessed to the murder?

Carradine: There was no confession.

Grant: What?

Carradine: There wasn't one.

Grant: But every history book I've read states that he confessed to the murder of the boys. Even Nurse Darrell is convinced of it.

Carradine: Oh, there are accounts of a confession, but no transcript. Nothing was published at the time.

Grant: So, when was it published.

Carradine: Henry's personal biographer, Virgil, later published an account of the murder of the princes in the tower, but that came after Tyrrell had been beheaded. There is no record of Tyrrell making a confession before he was executed. None at all.

Grant: Then he can't have confessed. If he had done, then it is just impossible that Henry would not make it public before the execution. And if it was public, you would have found something.

Carradine: That point is settled then?

Grant: What was the name of that constable? The one that was supposed to have released the boys to Tyrrell.

Carradine: Brackenbury.

Grant: Yes. What happened to him?

Carradine: Killed at Bosworth.

Grant: That's convenient.

Carradine: Indeed.

Grant: (*After a moment.*) I am satisfied. Richard had nothing to gain from murdering the boys whilst Henry had everything. The suspicion falls on him.

Carradine: The other player we have to consider is Stillington.

Grant: Ah yes, indeed. The Titulus Regius only came about due to his testimony that he had presided over the marriage of Edward to Eleanor Butler. Henry must have hated him.

Carradine: Henry had him locked up. Presumably to avoid him ever repeating his claim.

Grant: I suppose that would have been embarrassing now that Henry was claiming that the allegation was the Edward had been married to Elizabeth Lucy, something that it was easy to disprove. Did you find anything else?

Carradine: I did indeed.

Grant: Well?

Carradine: Something most satisfying.

Grant: (*Good humouredly.*) Come on, stop being smug, and spit it out.

Carradine: I found that break in the pattern that you wanted.

Grant: Excellent.

Carradine: It didn't come immediately. In the first months everyone did what you would expect them to do. Henry took over - not a word about the boys, got the Titulus Regius repealed and destroyed - not a word about the boys, got married to the boys' sister - not a word about the boys and charged Richard's followers with treason, thereby bringing a lot of forfeited estates into the kitty in one go.

That monk in Croyland, who we now know to be Morton, was angry about that, by the way. He wrote that it would be difficult for a king to raise an army if his followers risked losing their fortunes if they ended up on the losing side.

Grant: He had a point.

Carradine: He reckoned without his countrymen though. The treason charge caused such a scandal, Henry was forced to sign an act of parliament that said that no one could be charged with treason because they had fought on behalf of a defeated monarch. That aside, everything was as you would expect. Henry ascended to the throne in August 1485 and married his Elizabeth in January the following year. In September she gave birth to their first child. Her mother, Edward's widow, Elizabeth Woodville, was present at the birth and at the baptism. Then, six months later, we get the break in the pattern.

Grant: Go on.

Carradine: She was locked up.

Grant: Elizabeth Woodville? The boys' mother!

Carradine: Yes. She was shut up in a convent for the rest of her life.

Grant: How do you know she didn't go voluntarily?

Carradine: Henry stripped her of everything she owned.

Grant: Did he give a reason?

Carradine: Henry's pet biographer stated, "various considerations".

Grant: Is that a quote?

Carradine: Yes. "Various considerations".

Grant: What do you think was the real reason?

Carradine: Well, I have an idea. It's like this. In June that year...

Grant: What year?

Carradine: 1486, the year Henry married his Elizabeth. In June that year James Tyrrell was granted a pardon.

Grant: That is not all that extraordinary. We know that it was another twenty years before he was executed. The pardon will have been just because he'd been a supporter of Richard.

Carradine: Yes. But he was pardoned again in July.

Grant: What?

Carradine: It doesn't make any sense, does it?

Grant: He must have done something after the first pardon to warrant being pardoned again.

Carradine: That was my thinking too.

Grant: Good God.

Carradine: Do you see it?

Grant: Can it be true?

Carradine: You're the policeman.

Grant: When did the stories about the boys being missing first start appearing?

Carradine: Early in Henry's reign.

Grant: That's the thing that has always mystified historians, even the ones that paint Richard as a monster. If he was responsible, why was there no public outcry at the time? We've already established that the reason was because he wasn't responsible, but it bothered me where Tyrrell came into the matter. Now I think we have our answer.

Carradine: Say it out loud. I want to hear it from you.

Grant: Tyrrell did murder the princes in the tower. But not on the order of Richard. It was on the order of Henry.

Carradine: Who then immediately pardoned him for it.

Grant: And sent the boy's mother off to a convent.

Carradine: It is possible she never even knew what happened to the boys.

Grant: Which explains the mystery around Tyrrell's confession.

Carradine: Yes. Because, if he had confessed, it would have been to murdering the boys on orders given to him by Henry.

Grant: So, either there was no confession or there was one that Henry would have had destroyed.

Carradine: Then have his pet biographer make up a confession that suited him better.

Grant: I wonder how Henry explained the boys' disappearance to his wife. Perhaps he told her the truth.

Carradine: Henry? Never!

Grant: One question. Tyrrell was pardoned in June and then again in July. How soon after that did he receive his appointment in France? The Constable of Calais.

Carradine: I knew you were going to ask me that. It was almost immediately. In that same year.

Grant: That's the final nail. Tyrrell wasn't just pardoned, he was rewarded.

Carradine: Case concluded?

Grant: I think we've enough to go to court. Or, in this case, for you to write your book. Unless you have already started it. Have you?

Carradine: I've had a few thoughts but not written anything down yet. That is why I wanted to speak to you before I started. With your permission I would like to write it just as it happened. With me coming to see you and us applying police techniques.

Grant: Just as it should be. Perhaps when you are finished you should send a copy to Cuthbert Oliphant. Let him see how history should be interpreted.

Carradine: Poor Atlanta thinks that I have abandoned her. She was a bit cross last night when I told her that, for the first time in my life, I had found something important to do. A silly thing for me to have said, when I think about it. Of course, Atlanta is the most important thing in my life, but this book could be the real making of me. Would you mind if I dedicated it to you?

Grant: You might be better dedicating it to your father.

Carradine: I've no intention of using the dedication to flatter anyone. I wouldn't have started on this thing if it wasn't for you, and I would like to use the dedication to acknowledge that.

Grant: Well, in that case, I would be honoured.

Carradine: I forgot to ask you how you are feeling.

Grant: A bit sore but I walked to the window and back before you arrived.

Carradine: You are making progress, then.

Grant: They say I should be able to go home in a few days

Carradine: That's wonderful. Hey! I could drive you home if you like. I mean, if that's not an imposition.

Grant: That's very kind of you. I was going to ask my sergeant, but I shouldn't take him away from his duties.

Carradine: Give me a call when you get the green light.

Grant: I will. Thank you.

Carradine: Well, I had better go to see if I can smooth Atlanta's ruffled feathers. I'll see you in a couple of days.

Grant: I hope so, Brent.

Blackout.

Scene Ten

A few days later. Grant is sat in the chair, dozing. Marta enters carrying a book.

Marta: Oh Alan, darling. You're not even dressed.

Grant: What's that? Oh, hello Marta.

Marta: I thought you were going home today.

Grant: I am. I'm just waiting for Nurse Darrell to bring my release papers.

Marta: You are not being released from prison, Alan.

Grant: Aren't I?

Marta: And is Nurse Darrell also bringing you some clothes?

Grant: No, that's Bedbug. I mean Nurse Ingham. There seems to be some strange hierarchical arrangement that could only exist in a hospital. What's that you have there.

Marta: Oh, I took it out of the library when I returned More. I thought it might interest you, but I suppose you'll be getting back to real cases now. I was going to just take it straight back to the library but then I thought I might as well give you the choice as I was coming here anyway.

Grant: Yes, why are you here?

Marta: That's not very friendly.

Grant: Sorry, darling. I mean, how did you know I was leaving today.

Marta: Brent told me. He's got a big old Austin so I thought I could ride back with you and help you settle in at home.

Grant: That's very kind of you. Let's have a look at the book then. (*Marta passes him the book.*) Historic Doubts on the life and Reign of Richard III. Well, well. Good lord. Horace Walpole.

Marta: Do you know him?

Grant: Wasn't he the son of Robert Walpole, the prime minister? Yes. It says here on the back.

Carradine enters, looking downbeat.

Carradine: Hello Mr. Grant, Miss Hallard.

Grant: Hello Brent. Something up? You don't look very happy.

Carradine: We've come unstuck, I'm afraid.

Grant: Unstuck? What's come unstuck?

Carradine: Everything.

Grant: What? Have you uncovered evidence the boys disappeared whilst under the care of Richard?

Carradine: Worse than that. Much worse than that. Now I'll never write that book.

Grant: Why not?

Carradine: Because it isn't news. Everyone knows that Richard didn't kill those boys.

Grant: What do you mean "everyone knows"?

Carradine: Someone called Buck wrote about it in the seventeenth century. Then Horace Walpole in the eighteenth.

Grant: (*Holding up the book.*) This, you mean?

Carradine: (*Shocked.*) You knew?

Grant: I promise you that Miss Hallard has only just given me this. I had no knowledge of its existence two minutes ago.

Carradine: Well, listen to this. (*He takes the book and opens it at the last page.*) "Henry's character is so much worse and more hateful than Richard's, that we may well believe Henry, not Richard, probably put to death young princes".

Grant: I wouldn't argue with that, except that there is no "may well believe" about it.

Carradine: After Walpole came someone called Markham.

Grant: When was this?

Carradine: The turn of the century.

Grant: Well, there you are. Nothing in the last 50 years. There is no reason why you shouldn't add to the pile.

Carradine: But it won't be the same.

Grant: How do you mean?

Carradine: It won't be a Great Discovery.

Grant: (*Sharply.*) Oh, come on, boy.

Carradine looks like he is about to cry.

Marta: Alan! When did you become so heartless?

Grant: I'm sorry, I'm sorry. I didn't mean to upset you. But Great Discoveries don't grow on trees, you know.

Having said that, it doesn't mean that you can't lead a crusade.

Carradine: A crusade?

Grant: Yes. If people have been saying for three hundred and fifty years that Richard did not kill his nephews, but all the history books still say that he did, then you should do something about it.

Carradine: But why should anyone take any notice of me?

Grant: Because you have passion. I'm not saying it will be easy. It will certainly be an uphill battle to convince the British public.

Carradine: Because I've not written a book before, you mean?

Grant: No, that doesn't matter at all. Most people's first books are their best anyway; it's the one they wanted most to write. No, I meant that all the people who've never read a history book since they left school will feel themselves qualified to pontificate about what you've written. They'll accuse you of whitewashing Richard; "whitewashing" has a derogatory sound that "rehabilitation" hasn't, so they'll call it whitewashing. A few will look it up the Encyclopedia Britannica and feel vindicated that it confirms what they believe to be true. And the serious historians won't even bother to notice you.

Carradine: By God, I will make them notice me.

Marta: That's the spirit.

Carradine: This is not speculation or theory. It is a logical conclusion based on actual evidence. Let them ignore that at their peril.

Grant: Good man.

Carradine: To think that I nearly threw all my notes on the fire.

Grant: What stopped you?

Carradine: It's an electric fire.

Marta giggles.

Grant: Speaking of notes, I have one for you. (*Passing Carradine a sheet from his notepad.*) I summed it all up as a policeman would. I thought it might be helpful to you.

Carradine: (*Reading.*)

RICHARD III.

Previous Record:

Good. Has excellent record in public service, and good reputation in private life. Salient characteristic as indicated by his actions: good sense.

In the matter of the presumed crime:

(a) He did not stand to benefit; there were nine other heirs to the house of York, including three males.
(b) There is no contemporary accusation.
(c) The boys' mother continued on friendly terms with

him until his death, and her daughters attended Palace festivities.

(d) He showed no fear of the other heirs of York, providing generously for their upkeep and granting all of them their royal state.

(e) His own right to the crown was unassailable, approved by Act of Parliament and public acclamation; the boys were out of the succession and of no danger to him.

(f) If he had been nervous about disaffection then the person to have got rid of was not the two boys, but the person who really was next in succession to him: young Warwick. Whom he publicly created his heir when his own son died.

HENRY VII

Previous Record:

An adventurer, living at foreign courts. Son of an ambitious mother. Nothing known against his private life. No public office or employment. Salient characteristic as indicated by his actions: subtlety.

In the matter of the presumed crime:

(a) It was of great importance to him that the boys should not continue to live. By repealing the Act acknowledging the children's illegitimacy, he made the elder boy King of England, and the younger boy the next heir.

(b) In the Act which he brought before Parliament he accused Richard of the conventional tyranny and cruelty but made no mention of the two young Princes. The conclusion is inevitable that at that time the two boys were alive and their whereabouts known.

(c) The boys' mother was deprived of her living and consigned to a nunnery eighteen months after his succession.

(d) He took immediate steps to secure the persons of all the other heirs to the crown, and kept them in close arrest until he could with the minimum of scandal get rid of them.

(e) He had no right whatever to the throne. Since the death of Richard, young Warwick was next in line to the throne.

Marta: Once a policeman, always a policeman.

Carradine: This is very useful. Thank you, Mr. Grant, it will help me remember the pertinent points.

Grant: Well, if you ever want to check anything with me you are always free to call.

Carradine: Won't you be too busy with real investigations.

Grant: I can always make time for you. I don't think I have ever enjoyed an investigation more than I have enjoyed this one.

Darrell enters.

Darrell: Everything's sorted. You can go when you are ready. Oh, you are not dressed.

Grant: I think Bedbug has stolen my clothes in retaliation for all the teasing.

Darrell: And what are you going to do with all these books?

Grant: Mr. Carradine can take Oliphant back and your history books are somewhere in that pile. The rest can go in the hospital library.

Darrell: Thank you. Shall I threw away this horrible picture?

Carradine: I'll take it, if you don't mind.

Grant: Before that, would you do me a favour, Nurse Darrell?

Darrell: Of course.

Grant: Take the picture over to the window where the light is best and take a proper look at it. Look at it for as long as it takes to take a pulse.

Marta: I'll time you.

Darrell takes the picture to the window and studies it.

Marta: (*Looking at her watch.*) Go.

Fifteen seconds pass.

Marta: (*Looking at her watch.*) Fifteen seconds.

Another fifteen seconds pass.

Marta: (*Looking at her watch.*) Thirty seconds.

Ingham enters.

Ingham: What's going on?

Grant: Shhh.

Another fifteen seconds pass.

Marta: (*Looking at her watch.*) Forty-five seconds.

Ingham: Why are you timing Nurse Darrell?

Another fifteen seconds pass.

Marta: That's it. One minute.

Grant: Well?

Darrell: Funny. When you look at it for a little, it's really quite a nice face, isn't it?

Ingham: (*Walking over and taking the photo.*) He still looks like he is constipated to me.

All: Bedbug!

Ingham: Nurse Ingham!

End

Milton Keynes UK
Ingram Content Group UK Ltd.
UKHW010633061123
432055UK00001B/139